The Quest for Personal Best
Individual Sports

Lisa Greathouse

The Quest for Personal Best
Individual Sports

Publishing Credits

Editorial Director
Dona Herweck Rice

Associate Editors
James Anderson
Torrey Maloof

Editor-in-Chief
Sharon Coan, M.S.Ed.

Creative Director
Lee Aucoin

Illustration Manager
Timothy J. Bradley

Publisher
Rachelle Cracchiolo, M.S.Ed.

Science Consultant
Scot Oschman, Ph.D.

Teacher Created Materials
5301 Oceanus Drive
Huntington Beach, CA 92649-1030
http://www.tcmpub.com

ISBN 978-1-4333-0306-7

Table of Contents

Sports: Team vs. Individual 4

The Science of Sports 6

Velocity and Acceleration 12

What Will Happen Next? 20

Pushing the Limits 26

Appendices 28

- Lab: Seat Belt Safety 28
- Glossary 30
- Index 31
- Scientists Then and Now 32
- Image Credits 32

Sports: Team vs. Individual

What is the first thing you think of when you think of sports? Is it baseball? Soccer? Basketball? These are all team sports. Maybe you have a favorite team. You might even play on a team. Some kids start playing team sports before they begin going to school!

But team sports are not right for everyone. Some people prefer individual sports. These are sports that you do on your own. Golf, swimming, and skating are some examples. You can compete in these sports or play them for fun. How well you do depends on you.

Sometimes teams are made up of people in individual sports. Think of a swim team or a track team. These teams are still individual sports because each athlete usually performs without other team members. Each athlete gets to shine while still being part of a team.

Sports

Here are some examples of team sports and individual sports. What's your favorite?

Individual Sports	Team Sports
auto racing	baseball
bowling	basketball
cycling	football
golf	hockey
gymnastics	soccer
martial arts	softball
running	waterpolo
skateboarding	
skating	
skiing	
swimming	
tennis	
wrestling	

The Science of Sports

There are athletes in both team *and* individual sports who want to do more than just win. They want to be *the best* at their sports. They want to set records. They want to be the fastest, strongest, or most **agile** (AJ-uhl).

Science is a big part of sports. Every kind of sport involves **motion**. Motion is how and where something moves. Without motion, a skateboarder would never land a trick. A volleyball player would never spike a ball. A golfer would never make a putt. In fact, nothing much would *ever* happen! Motion is always around us. Everything in the world moves. Earth moves. That means everything on Earth is moving, too!

But things don't move on their own. They need a **force** to make them move. A force is a push or a pull that causes movement. You use forces all the time. On a bicycle, the force of your muscles moves your bones. Your bones make the pedals move. When you kick a ball, the force makes the ball fly or roll.

A Great Athlete

What does it take to become a great athlete? Some say that being fast is the most important thing. Others say it is all about how strong or **flexible** you are, or how quickly you can react. Being competitive is a big factor, too. These skills are all tested in the **decathlon** (duh-KATH-lon). This is an event that combines 10 track and field races. Many people call the winner the "World's Greatest Athlete."

"The Greatest"

Not too many athletes receive the Presidential Medal of Freedom. But in 2005, boxer Muhammad Ali did. Ali is nicknamed "The Greatest," and he has been called the best athlete of the 20th century. But he has also been a champion out of the ring. He has worked for world peace, aid for poor countries, and civil rights for African Americans. He has raised money for medical research. He has bravely fought his own weakening illness. Ali's courage continues to inspire millions.

Who Wins?

Measurements (MEZH-ur-muhnts) are used to figure out the winner of most individual sporting events. Sometimes speed is what is measured, as in a swim meet. Sometimes it is distance, as in the long jump. In many sports, the winner of a competition is decided by a fraction of a second or in millimeters!

Using Science to Improve Your Game

The best athletes in the world train for hours every day. They work with coaches. They eat healthy food. They get plenty of rest. These are some of the things that make them so good at their sports.

But great athletes also understand how **physics** (FIZ-iks) affects how well they do. Physics is the science of force and motion. Athletes can run faster, jump higher, and have better balance if they understand how physics can help them.

A good example is the high jump. Jumpers used to run and then jump over the bar by throwing one leg over and then the other. But it takes a lot of **energy** to jump that way. An athlete named Dick Fosbury found a better way. He twisted his body so that he went over head first with his back next to the bar. This shifted his weight as it went over the bar. It also took less energy. He won the Olympic gold medal in the high jump that year. Most high jumpers today use the "Fosbury Flop."

Olympic Games

The first Olympic Games can be traced to 776 B.C. Every four years, athletes from all over Greece came to compete in a great festival. At first, only men were allowed. Today, male and female athletes from all over the world compete in more than 400 events!

Lightning Bolt!

At the 2008 Olympic Games, Usain Bolt of Jamaica (below) became the fastest sprinter of all time. Bolt won gold medals in three events and set Olympic and world records. People everywhere call him "Lightning Bolt."

Let Your Lean Do The Work!

The fastest runners pay attention to how they place their bodies. They know how to use **gravity** (GRAV-ah-tee) to make them run faster. Gravity is the force that holds us on the ground. It keeps us from floating into space.

Lean forward as you run. Then the force of gravity will pull you forward, and you will run faster. Just remember to lean from your ankles and not your waist. Also, bend your arms and legs while running. You will use less energy. You will be able to run a longer distance.

Champion

Jackie Joyner-Kersee (left) is one of the greatest female track stars in history. She won three Olympic medals in the **heptathlon** (hep-TATH-luhn). It is one of the hardest races. It combines seven events, including hurdles, the high jump, and the shot put.

A Big Job for the Big Toe

The size of your toes can offer a clue about your ability in sports. For some people, their second toes are longer than their big toes. But if your big toe is longer, you have a natural advantage for sports like running and skiing. That is because you can lean your body weight into it. Your big toe can put out about twice as much force as your second toe!

Velocity and Acceleration

Sports are all about speed. Speed is how far something moves in a given time. In most sports, it is the athlete who needs to be fast. In some sports, it is the ball. Many sports depend on how fast the athlete swings the bat, racket, or club.

Acceleration (ak-sel-uh-RAY-shuhn) is more than just moving fast. It is a change in speed. When you take off on skates, you accelerate. That is because you change your speed. When a golfer swings a club, the ball can accelerate 100 times faster than a sports car can!

Velocity (vuh-LOS-i-tee) is a change in speed *and* direction. When a race car slows to go around a turn on the track, it changes velocity.

Did You Know?

Tiger Woods began to play golf when he was just two years old.

Tiger Woods

When people think of golf, they often think about Tiger Woods. Tiger is one of the top golfers in the world. He was the youngest player ever to win all four major golf tournaments. He has inspired people all over the world to take up the sport.

BMX bike

mountain bikes

tandem bike

Tour de France

The Tour de France is one of the most famous bicycle races in the world. About 200 athletes compete in the three-week bike race across France every year. It covers 3,219 kilometers (2,000 miles). Riders compete to wear the coveted first place yellow jersey.

A Bicycle for Everyone

Many people ride bicycles for fun. Some use them for transportation. But cycling is also a sport. There are bike races on tracks, roads, and through mountains. BMX cyclists perform tricks on their bikes.

A bike is called a human-powered vehicle. It gets all its energy from the person riding it. You will go faster if you pedal harder.

The amount of force that is needed to move something depends on the object's **mass**. Mass is the amount of "stuff"—or matter—that makes up the object. It takes more force to move a bike that has two people on it than a bike that has just one.

Each kind of cycling has its own kind of bike. Racing bicycles are made from light metals. Lighter bikes are easier to move because they have less mass. Different kinds of bikes also have different kinds of wheels, gears, and pedals. Some racing bikes do not even have brakes!

What a Drag!

Aerodynamics (air-oh-dye-NAM-iks) is the way the air flows around a moving object. The way a cyclist sits on his or her bike affects how fast the bike can move. If you sit up straight in the seat, your body will fight the force of the air against it. That slows you down. If you bend at the waist with your hands on low handlebars, the air does not hit as many parts of your body. That lets you go faster.

Cyclists are not the only athletes who have to work against the wind. Air movement can also slow down runners, swimmers, and racecar drivers. Have you ever tried swimming laps in a pool? If you have, then you know how much energy it takes. To move through water, a swimmer must push on fluid that is almost 800 times as dense as air. The force that slows you down in the pool is called **drag**. It is the resistance against your body. When you kick your legs, it keeps you near the surface. This reduces drag and helps to speed you up.

Swimming Like a Fish

Michael Phelps is one of the fastest swimmers of all time. He first made the Olympic team when he was only 15. He was also the youngest male swimmer to set a world record. He won a record eight gold medals at the 2008 Olympics. Experts say that Phelps is built to swim. He is six-foot-seven-inches tall and has size 14 feet!

Wind Tunnel

Cyclists and bicycle makers can use wind tunnels to test new ways to cut through the wind. A wind tunnel at the Massachusetts Institute of Technology has huge fans that blast winds at 48 kilometers (30 miles) per hour!

The Speed Suit

A fraction of a second can make all the difference in a race. So, top athletes wear clothing that will not slow them down. Runners, swimmers, and skaters are just a few of the kinds of athletes who wear special speed suits. The material is skintight. That makes the athletes' bodies more aerodynamic.

The Friction Factor

When it comes to speed, **friction** (FRIK-shuhn) is not your friend—until you want to stop!

Friction is a force that creates drag and slows you down. There is friction whenever things rub against one another. The rougher the two surfaces are, the more friction there is between them.

Think about how it feels to walk across a smooth floor in your socks. You can probably just glide across the floor. Both surfaces are smooth. But when you put on your running shoes, there is more friction. Your shoes have "sticking power" to the floor. Athletes who rely on speed try to lower friction and keep their surfaces smooth.

Some snowboarders and skiers wax the bottom of their boards or skis. In that way, there is less friction with the ice or snow.

snowboarder

What Will Happen Next?

Roger Federer

Swiss tennis player Roger Federer just keeps breaking records. He is often called the best tennis player in history. Experts say that the amazing speed and force of his swing are what make him a champion.

Some people think that tennis is a boring sport to watch. It is just two people hitting a ball back and forth. Right? Wrong. Every time the racket hits the ball, something different happens. The way the ball travels depends on the force and angle of the racket. It relies on the way the ball bounces on the court. It depends on whether there is a "spin" on the ball. The spin makes it move in a way you would not expect. A gust of wind can even send the ball in a different direction!

A lot also depends on the kind of racket being used. A lightweight racket is easy and quick to swing. But if it is *too* light, it may not be able to handle the impact of the ball. In some tennis matches, the ball zooms across the court at speeds over 225 kilometers (140 miles) per hour!

Sister Act

Sisters Venus and Serena Williams started playing tennis before they even started school. They grew into two of the greatest tennis players of all time. They both have Olympic gold medals and Grand Slam titles. Venus can serve the ball at 204 kilometers (127 miles) per hour!

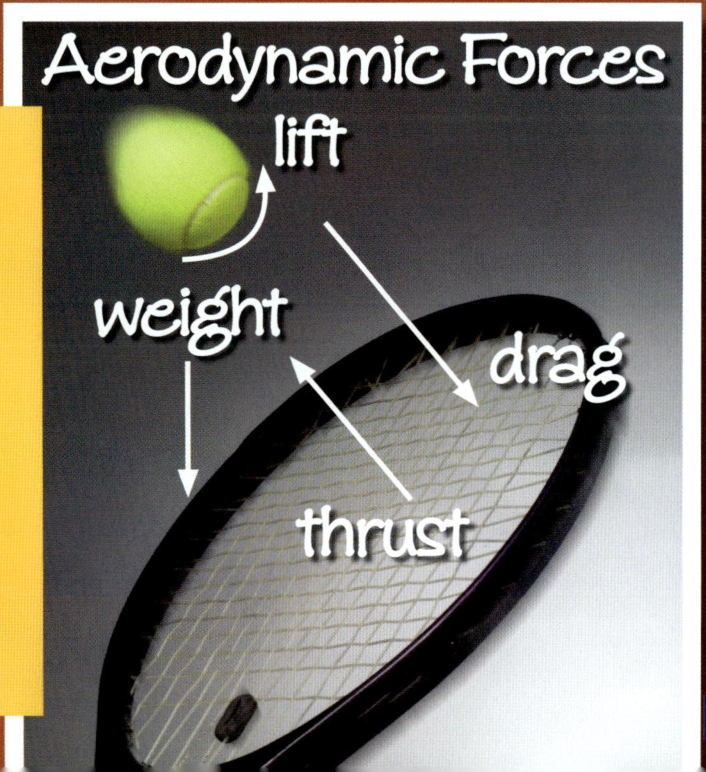

- **Thrust** is the force made by a racket on the ball. It pushes the ball through the air.
- The **lift** of the tennis ball begins when spin is applied by the racket.
- The ball's **weight** is the force created by gravity. It pulls it down to Earth.
- Drag slows the ball down. It is caused by friction and air resistance.

Finding Your Balance

Think of a sport that takes great balance. Did gymnastics come to mind? Maybe that is because many gymnasts perform on a balance beam. Gymnastics is just one sport that requires balance.

Balance is a big part of our lives. We need balance to walk and run. We also need balance just to sit and stand. If it were not for your balance, you would fall over! Balance has a lot to do with your **center of mass.** The center of mass is the point at which an object is balanced.

For humans, the center of mass is usually right behind their belly buttons when they are standing straight. But if they change positions, their centers of mass change. Think about standing on one foot. You have to shift your weight so that you do not fall over. That is because your center of mass changes when you lift a foot off the ground.

Nadia Comaneci

In the 1976 Olympic Games, Romanian gymnast Nadia Comaneci (koh-muh-NEECH) (right) became the first gymnast to earn a perfect score of 10. The scoreboards were not even equipped to show a 10 at that time. So, they showed a 1.0 instead!

The gymnast balances her body from her center of mass.

Tony Hawk

Tony Hawk (right) may be the most famous skateboarder in history. He was just nine when his brother changed his life: He gave Tony his first board. Tony set his mind on being the best. By age 16, Tony was the world champion.

Skateboarding Stunts

The first skateboards were nothing more than wooden planks on roller skate wheels. Skateboarders would just try to keep from falling or crashing into something! Today, they fly through the air on their skateboards. They do flips and turns at top speeds. Have you ever wondered how they do it? The answer has a lot to do with physics.

First of all, skateboards are now made from new materials. They are designed for speed. New boards curve up at the edges. That gives the rider more control. Skateboarders use that control to do tricks that seem impossible.

Doin' an Ollie

The "ollie" is the most popular skateboard trick. It is a jump that looks like the skater has the board attached to his or her shoes. To do an ollie, the skater slams down hard with a foot on the back of the board. This makes the board bounce up. When the board is in the air, the skater slides his or her front foot forward. The friction between the foot and the board drags the board higher. Then, gravity takes over. The board and skater land flat on the ground.

Food Guide Pyramid

If you are eating healthy, well-balanced meals and snacks, you are probably getting the energy you need to perform well in sports. These are foods you should be eating every day.

Grains	Vegetables	Fruits	Milk	Meat and Beans
Make half your grains whole.	Vary your veggies.	Focus on fruits.	Crave calcium-rich foods.	Go lean with protein.

Pushing the Limits

Sports are a great way to have fun and stay active. No matter what your favorite sport is, there is always room to improve your game. It helps to have a goal. Do you want to be the best skateboarder in your neighborhood? Or the fastest runner at school? Do you want to be an Olympic athlete one day? Or maybe you just want to learn a new sport for fun. There are so many choices!

Once you set a goal, you need to have a plan for getting there. Olympic athletes train for hours every day. You do not have to go that far. But it is a good idea to practice several times a week. It is also great to have someone to help you. A coach, relative, or friend who knows the sport are all good choices. It is always easier to reach your goals when you have someone cheering you on. But the most important thing is that you believe in yourself!

Man as Machine

You may not think of your body as a **machine**. But that is exactly what it is. Just like any machine, your body needs energy to perform its best. That energy comes from the food we eat. So, sometimes you feel tired if you skip meals. The healthier you eat, the better your body performs.

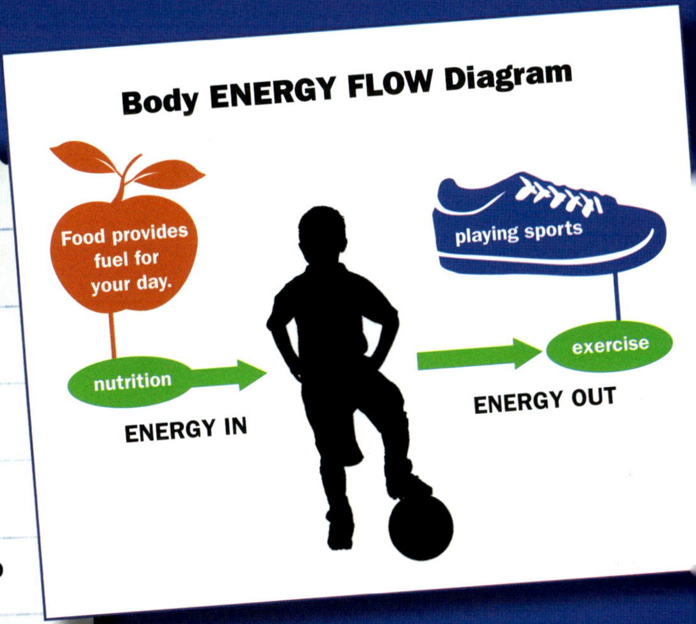

Lab: Seat Belt Safety

When riding in a car, you are moving at the same speed as the car. It is important to wear your seat belt! If the car has to stop suddenly, the seat belt will keep you from flying out of your seat.

Materials

- piece of stiff cardboard, at least 45 cm x 30 cm (18 inches x 12 inches)
- two books, each about 2.5 cm (1 inch) thick
- masking tape
- pencil
- piece of modeling clay
- small toy car
- piece of ribbon, 30 cm (12 inches) long
- ruler
- stopwatch

Procedure:

1. Take the piece of cardboard and place one end of it on the edge of one of the books, creating a ramp.
2. Tape the other end of the cardboard to a table or onto the floor.
3. Tape the pencil to the table about two toy-car lengths from the taped end of the cardboard.
4. Use the clay to make a small figure, such as a snowman, about 5 centimeters (2 inches) tall.

5. Flatten the bottom of the clay figure and rest it on the car's hood. Do not press the clay onto the car.

6. Position the car and clay figure at the raised end of the cardboard.

7. At the same time you release the car to roll down the cardboard, start the stopwatch. Stop the stopwatch when the car hits the pencil. Record the time. Also record how many inches the clay figure lands from the pencil. Use a table like the one shown below.

8. Use the ribbon to tie the clay figure to the car. Then repeat steps 5 through 7. The clay figure should stay on the car.

9. Now, stack two books instead of one under the cardboard to make the ramp steeper. Repeat the experiment.

10. Compare the times and distances. Why are the distances and times different?

	One–Book Ramp	**Two–Book Ramp**
Car Speed (with loose clay figure, in seconds)		
Car Speed (with tied-on clay figure, in seconds)		
Clay Figure Landing (inches from pencil)		

Glossary

aerodynamics—the study of movement of air

acceleration—a change in speed

agile—quick

center of mass—the point at which an object is balanced

decathlon—sports event combining 10 track and field races

drag—force that acts against the movement of an object

energy—the power to do work

flexible—bendable

force—a push or pull that makes things move

friction—the force that acts on surfaces in contact and slows them down

gravity—a force that attracts things to each other

heptathlon—sports event combining seven track and field races

lift—a force that raises

machine—something that uses movement to make work easier

mass—the amount of matter something is made of

motion—a change in position

physics—the science of force and motion

thrust—a force that moves an object

velocity—the rate of change in speed and direction

weight—a result of the force of gravity

Index

acceleration, 12
aerodynamics, 16, 18, 21
Ali, Muhammad, 7
Armstrong, Lance, 14
bicycle, 6, 15–17
Bolt, Usain, 10
center of mass, 22
Comaneci, Nadia, 22
decathlon, 7
drag, 16, 21
energy, 9–10, 16, 26–27
Federer, Roger, 20
Food Guide Pyramid, 26
force, 6, 9–11, 15–16, 19–21
Fosbury, Dick, 9
friction, 19, 21, 25
gravity, 10, 21, 25
Hawk, Tony, 24
Joyner-Kersee, Jackie, 11
machine, 27
mass, 15, 22
motion, 6, 9
ollie, 25
Olympics, 9–11, 16, 21, 22, 27
Phelps, Michael, 16
speed suit, 18
Tour de France, 14
velocity, 12
Williams, Serena, 21
Williams, Venus, 21
Woods, Tiger, 12–13

Scientists Then and Now

Wernher von Braun
(1912–1977)

Human beings are forever on a quest to excel. Wernher von Braun was no exception. He was born in Germany and became a leading figure in the development of rockets. He helped to develop rockets for America's space program. He was the chief engineer for the *Saturn V* rocket that propelled the *Apollo* spacecraft to the moon. He was also a big part of getting public support for the whole space program.

Ron Ayers
(1932–)

In school in England, Ron Ayers studied planes, spaceships, and flight. After college, he worked to help make airplanes and missiles fly better. Eventually, he retired from his job. But he was still curious. He studied more about flight and speed. Then he worked with a group of people to break the sound barrier with a land vehicle. It was the fastest land vehicle ever at 1,228 kilometers (763 miles) per hour!

Image Credits

Cover Ben Heys/Shutterstock; p.1 Ben Heys/Shutterstock; p.4 Galina Barskaya/Shutterstock; p.4-5 Ronen/Shutterstock; p.5 Gert Johannes Jacobus Vrey/Shutterstock; p.5(right) Laurin Rinder/Shutterstock; p.6-7 Popperfoto/Getty Images; p.7 Image of Sport/Newscom; p.8 c40/ZUMA Press/Newscom; p.9 The Print Collector/Alamy; p.10 i30/ZUMA Press/Newscom; p.10-11 Konstantin Sutyagin/Shutterstock; p.11 Tony Duffy/Getty Images; p.12-13(top) CHEN WEI SENG/Shutterstock; p.12-13 Adrian Dennis/AFP/GETTY IMAGES/ Newscom; p.14(left) Suzanne Tucker/Shutterstock; p.14(middle) Marcel Jancovic/Shutterstock; p.14(right) Juriah Mosin/Shutterstock; p.14-15(bottom) Friedemann Vogel/Bongarts/Getty Images; p.14-15 kRie/Shutterstock; p.17 Andy Sacks/Getty Images; p.17(bottom) Tim Clary/AFP/GETTY IMAGES/Newscom; p.18-19 Toshifumi Kitamura/AFP/Newscom; p.19 Lisovskaya Natalia/Shutterstock; p.20 Adrian Dennis/AFP/Getty Images/Newscom; p.21 Carl de Souza/AFP/Getty Images/Newscom; p.21(bottom) Dusanzidar/Dreamstime; p.22-23 Sports Illustrated/Getty Images; p.23 Jiang Dao Hua/Shutterstock; p.24 Rick Rickman/NewSport/Corbis; p.24-25 Romanchuck Dimitry/Shutterstock; p.25 LANBO/Shutterstock; p.26 Jupiterimages Corporation; p.26 gordana/Shutterstock; p.26 Norman Chan/Shutterstock; p.26 Elnur/Shutterstock; p.26 Shutterstock; p.26 Shutterstock; p.28 jaddingt/Shutterstock; p.29(top) Eimantas Buzas/Shutterstock; p.32(left) NASA; p.32(right) Rick Reason